TALES from the CUBAN EMPIRE

TALES
from the
CUBAN EMPIRE

ANTONIO JOSÉ PONTE

Translated from the Spanish
by Cola Franzen

CITY LIGHTS BOOKS
San Francisco

First published as *Cuentos de todas partes del Imperio*, Editions
Deleatur, Angers, France, 2000.
Translation copyright © 2002 by Cola Franzen

Editor: Nancy J. Peters
Typesetting: Harvest Graphics
Cover design: Amy Trachtenberg and Robin Raschke

Library of Congress Cataloging-in-Publication Data

Ponte, Antonio José, 1964–
    [Cuentos de todas partes del imperio. English]
    Tales from the Cuban empire / by Antonio José Ponte ;
translated from the Spanish by Cola Franzen.
        p.   cm.
    ISBN 0-87286-407-3 (pbk.)
        I. Title

PQ7390.P59 C8313 2002
863'.64—dc21   2002073891

CITY LIGHTS BOOKS are edited by Lawrence Ferlinghetti
and Nancy J. Peters and published at the City Lights Bookstore,
261 Columbus Avenue, San Francisco CA 94133.
www.citylights.com

ACKNOWLEDGMENTS

The original volume, *Cuentos de todas partes del Imperio*, with illustrations by Ramón Alejandro, was published by Éditions Deleatur, Colección Baralanube, Angers, France, in December 2000, under the direction of Ramón Alejandro.

Tales from the Cuban Empire could never have been done without the constant, meticulous, enthusiastic cooperation of the author. He has answered my many queries with unfailing patience and good humor. To him my most heartfelt thanks. A special debt of gratitude is owed to Dick Cluster, Mark Schafer, and Noemí Escandell, whose explanations, corrections, and suggestions were invaluable. My thanks to Alicia Borinsky who helped me untie some knots, and to my husband, Wolfgang Franzen, for too many reasons to list here. Robert Sharrard and Nancy J. Peters at City Lights have championed this project from the beginning, and have contributed so much that I am at a loss to express the full extent of my appreciation, admiration, and gratitude I feel for them. And thank you also, Nancy, for your usual expert editing. To all, mil gracias.

CONTENTS

PROLOGUE

PLEA FOR THE HEAD OF SCHEHERAZADE

"When men foregather from the uttermost ends of the Empire, they have a right to be riotous," Rudyard Kipling wrote in one of his stories about the English in India. And for the stories that follow, the same statement might apply.

They tell of lives of travelers and wanderings of tribes. They come from a butcher shop in the Chinese Quarter, from the court of Queen Elizabeth II of England, from the women's restroom in an airport, from the snows of Russia, from a strange subterranean city . . . From all corners of the Empire.

A book as rich as *The Thousand and One Nights* justifies its diversity thanks to a girl who tells stories to save her life. This short volume, for its part, has as its only justification the fact that the Empire exists. Just as the narrators of these adventures could cross paths somewhere in the Imperial vastness, so these five stories have come together here.

Cigarettes lit, coffee served, the rather sad news of each corner from which the travelers come now divulged, it quickly becomes apparent that the Empire consists only of that bitter aroma rising from their cups, the pungent smoke of the tobacco, the words, the music. Nothing but air, after all. Its very lack of consistency—usually a consolation in such cases—assures us that the Empire will never decline, if its founding is never completed.

Some scholars of *The Thousand and One Nights* speak of those whose profession it is to tell stories, *confabulatori nocturni*. Scheherazade (as well as the five who tell their stories here) is one of them and, as in the case of any creator of plots, it seems inevitable that she does so at the cost of her neck.

This prologue pleads for Scheherazade's head. Because whoever tells stories is always dependent on the whims or boredom of some king. And whoever writes them, on those of an unknown king: you, reader.

If the following pages start to bore you, slam the book shut, make Scheherazade's head roll.

TEARS IN THE CONGRÍ

Very seldom do newscasters here speak of other lands. Rarely does one hear what is happening in other countries. Our own is so vast, so many things occur in it, that interest in what goes on beyond our borders dwindles away. What's more, one can believe very little of world news, so that everything beyond our most distant outpost, the most distant guard in the most distant watchtower, becomes doubtful. I know because I'm the only member of my family who's traveled abroad; I lived outside for two years until the cold and atomic physics forced me to return.

I remember less and less of those student years, although the other night the whole experience flashed clearly before my eyes again. A television newscaster was describing the political instability of the world and my youngest brother, who is barely a year and a half old, caught a few words and repeated them in his fashion.

"Chechy chepra," he said, and we all burst out laughing.

Our first thought was how ludicrous it was for a rebel faction to have a title that seemed to be a tongue twister. The adventurers who gave themselves such a name, or at least accepted it, would neither kill nor be killed. If by any chance they were seeking a war, it would be a children's war.

"Che chepratist. . . chechens. . ." my youngest brother tried again.

In his customary way, my father made us understand that he would make a speech, and my mother's glance alerted us as usual: "He has to find something to do if he stays at home at night."

It was alcohol that taught him to speak with such bravado. From all his revelries he still kept the drunkeness of words and something that seemed amiss with his liver. Facing my mother, his seven sons, three daughters-in-law and two grandchildren, the old man set out to consider the advantages of living together in our own peaceful corner of the planet: a two-room apartment with neither balcony nor patio.

He raised the fist of his left hand.

"Teeming family," he exclaimed. And as if agreeing with him, the map of the country appeared on the screen behind his fist. The weatherman was starting his predictions. One of his gestures caused an entire front of clouds to move and cover the land, but my father was calling us to a greater illusion.

"Teeming family," he repeated with closed fist still raised.

Since there would be much more to hear, I made myself as comfortable as I could. And it was then I remembered the Congrí Heads.

The tribe we formed during our years of study appeared before me as if in a photo. One by one I saw their faces again.

Under that name we'd been students of atomic physics in a distant country. Atomic physics is a demanding science, and as for the cold, best not to speak of it at all. To this day, when I wake up in the morning, some of that cold stays in my bones. That's why, on Sunday afternoons, so far from home that you could see snow, it was perfect to be a Congrí Head. Whatever you might wish was right at hand: rum bought in import stores, a game of dominos, booming music, salsa dancing with bodies becoming more and more closely intertwined. There were girls, racy jokes, and chunks of fried pork with the totemic dish of the tribe, congrí, the special concoction of black beans and rice that we make at home.

We managed to serve it by hook or by crook. The little black eyes of the beans, shiny with pork fat as if each one had been polished separately — that was pure happiness. The beans shone like the eyes of a girl at the moment of making a promise. And their shine also allowed room for sighs, sobs, the pain of a heavy heart.

In a word, tears over the congrí.

To obtain black beans in the snow required fantastic negotiations. A Venezuelan brought us avocados as far as the Berlin Wall and, thanks to an importer of maté tea, we got shipments of *hierbabuena*, mint, to mix with the rum. From home we received sketches of the latest variations of dance steps. In short, we managed to live as if we had not left our homeland behind.

The cold, however, was all around us and, in order to become a true Congrí Head, you had to pass the snow test. The ceremony, more or less secret, consisted mainly in walking over the snow so as to flatten the enemy step by step. What was hard was the clothing required: feet in wooden-soled sandals such as we wear at home, the body covered only by pajama bottoms and undershirt, and on the head a woman's transparent nylon stocking. Scantily dressed and almost barefoot, the future Congrí Head was left with only one recourse, to advance shouting:

"Pan con lechón!" the roast pork sandwich we loved so much.

After the snow came the warmth — of music and rum and women. The steam from the new batch of congrí would burn the neophyte's face, he would dip his frozen arms into the big pot of rice and beans, then bury his head like being born backwards: now he was a Congrí Head.

Such a curious initiation rite went back to an ancient battle that occurred long before my time with the tribe. It began when a group of our girls returning one winter night to the students' residence were escaping less from the cold than from a gang pursuing them, guys who were carrying their impudence too far.

Since the girls belonged to our group, they were able to slip into the residence under the very noses of the gang, and once inside, shouted to the male dorm rooms the story of how they'd been insulted.

Added to the girls' cries were the gang's own war cries in an unknown jargon.

"Chechens," someone said, and the men of our tribe raced out.

The fight was quick. In a very few minutes the Chechens dispatched our group using blows of a type of martial arts as unknown to us as the very dialect they were jabbering.

With us, he who loses a fight among men also loses his step in the salsa dance and loses his chance at love with women. When all's said and done, these three activities — dancing, fighting, and sex — turn out to be the same: positions between bodies. The Congrí men had not known how to defend their women and in the future would not know how to satisfy them either on the dance floor or in bed. And down below, in the darkness of the snow, a gang of loud-mouthed strangers could bawl out their taunts against Congrí pride. All was lost.

Our men had formed a tribe to make their stay abroad bearable. They created the illusion that a foreign land did not surround them as the cold did, and now a handful of toughs took it upon themselves to teach the Congrí men that the place would never belong to them.

However, nobody counted on the fact that on the twelfth floor of the residence, in the very midst of the Congrí village, a man, a mulatto, was going through his daily exercise routine. Golomón was his surname, or his nickname, and if he hadn't heard anything of the fight, it was because he was wearing a woman's stocking pulled down low over his ears to make his hair lie close to his skull.

Golomón was opening and closing a pair of toning bands, stretching them out as far as his arms would go, swimming in the air with the grace of a manta ray through the water. When he saw the first of our wounded go by, without uttering one word, still in his sandals, he confronted the Chechens. The snow nipped his toes, the cold starched his pajama pants and his undershirt, but he wasted no energy on any declaration, and still wearing the woman's nylon cap, he swept through the Chechen mob, mowing them down with his toning bands.

The enemy, so sure of their martial arts skills up to then, couldn't get over their astonishment. As they fell and started crawling off in retreat, they asked by signs what that unknown weapon was called. Then, erect in his sandals, Golomón baptized his improvised sword with the first name that popped into his head.

"Pan con lechón!" he shouted to the snow and the night and the figures becoming smaller as they fled.

"Pan con lechón! Pan con lechón! Pan con lechón!" they repeated as well as their battered Chechen tongues could manage.

Needless to say, the pots started to steam, the bottles of rum were opened, and the salsa dancing lasted until the hesitant winter dawn appeared. Once again they had taught a gang of foreigners to have some respect. Respect, a new weapon, and three new words in their dialect that forever and ever, down to the grandchildren of their Chechen grandchildren, would mean fear, bitter defeat.

Years after that victory came my turn to take that walk through the snow, commemorating Golomón's foray. For a few years I was a Congrí Head. Later the cold and atomic physics did me in and I had to leave the tribe.

"You'll always be a Congrí," the last person to bid me good-bye assured me.

We'd made part of the journey together but now our paths diverged; I was going home and he to meet the Venezuelan about the avocados.

"You graduated walking in sandals through the snow," he added. "Always remember that."

As time went by, I stopped being a Congrí Head. The last time I was with the tribe, I was no longer one of them. They'd come back, each with a degree, and were celebrating on the rooftop of a house.

It was one of those summer days when the weatherman, magician though he might be, could not conjure up even one cloud for the weather report. And here was the entire tribe in the sun, among buckets of sea water and bottles of melted butter mixed with iodine. Only three blocks from the beach, but now used to great distances, those who'd walked barefoot through the snow acted as if it were impossible for them to cross those three blocks.

From the kitchen came the aroma of roast pork. From a tape player, a tune that everyone on the street was humming. They handed me a drink of a pink liquid they themselves had concocted with the same ingenuity that had made convoys of black beans move across foreign lands.

They strained the alcohol through a red scarf, sure sign that the cold had been left behind. And now that our best rum was exported, they were bent on having it brought back from the very same snow.

When my father, standing in front of the television, finished his lecture, little remained of the Congrí Heads. With their tattoos, their shields, and their lances, the tribe passed by like clouds across the weather map, with no one seeing them except for me. Sprawled on the sofa, an elbow poking into the ribs of one of my brothers, I thought that, without any doubt, the family was the best tribe.

However, I regretted not having paid more attention to that foreign news report on the television. Because ridiculous or not, the Chechen separatists would know the three words that Golomón had taught that gang. And it would be for sure their war cry:

"Pan con lechón!"

BECAUSE OF MEN

"If you've come this far, give yourself up," she said.

She was dragging a pile of suitcases that had passed through customs. She took out a lipstick and believing nobody else was in the restroom, talked aloud to herself.

I had just finished cleaning one of the stalls. I'm the woman with the dish and I collect what coins I can in this airport restroom. It was all the same to me whether she was a terrorist ready to turn herself in, or if she was into smuggling drugs or anything else in her pile of luggage. The coins in the dish would be the last foreign ones I'd collect if another scandal should erupt in my restroom.

She didn't turn toward me or even try to see me in the mirror. Judging by the stamps on her suitcases, she seemed to have gone through customs in every country and flown on every airline in the world.

"Could you leave me alone?" she asked in a near whisper.

I'd look like a beggar if I placed my table in the doorway. In this very restroom, on the other hand, I've often seen women trembling as they waited, hoping to board a plane. Let her cry all she wants. I moved the dish aside and offered her the chair. Then three girls came in with their bundles. They were talking about the night before, about some guys who'd made them dance even though they didn't know how.

"I'll pay you double what you usually get," she promised when the girls left. "So I can stay here."

I wondered aloud why she was hiding and she put a bill in the dish. I thanked her, kept the bill, and asked again.

"From men."

In that case she'd come to the perfect refuge.

I've also been afraid of men. In the long run, they make us all dance even though we might not know how. I have one son, he lives abroad, and one day I'm going to leave money in a dish like this one and go out the door to where the planes are.

"The evening he left," I told her, "I sat him down where you are so he'd speak frankly to me, look me in the eye, and say if he would come back or not."

That was the last time I felt afraid of a man.

"What did I care about the complaining women who had no restroom while I was talking to my son? Let them go outside to urinate! What did I care if I lost this job if the only person I had left in the world was leaving?

"I almost went crazy. I started to think that the people who travel, the luggage and the planes, were outside there to make me believe that other countries existed, when there was really only one, and it was this one."

"There are no others," she murmured.

I didn't understand whether she said there were others or were not.

"There are no others," she repeated in a louder voice.

Then I knew she was crazy.

She must have been about the same age as my son and I was glad she'd come back. That way, she'd make someone happy. Even if she had no family, even if her mother had died when she was a child and she had no home here any more. She was returning to her country and that was everything.

"I left years ago to get away from the men."

In novels people travel to escape things they don't like, love affairs, mostly. She'd done the same, but not because of one man. Because of men, all of them.

"One man who takes you far away can separate you from the others. He takes you to live in places where the cold and their upbringing make them different, where there seems to be no danger. But sooner or later, you will run into the first one who makes you glad to be speaking your own language, glad that you came from the same streets, a guy who reminds you of cer-

tain songs and wants to whisper them into your ear.
Then no precaution can help you.

"I married Stefan, we left, and it wasn't long before
just such a guy appeared who said we should get
together to escape such long winters and live the true
love of our lives, the love that nobody but one of our
own would know how to live. I couldn't stop listening
to him, believing his words. So I left with him for the
south. To feel once again that someone was capable of
carrying you to heaven and to hell in the same minute.

"We went to the south, I learned later, because of his
German wife's rheumatism. That explained why he
often left me alone and some nights slept elsewhere.

"I discovered her, so old and fat, and wanted to kill
her. But the two of us had to save ourselves from his
blows. Because he demanded that there be peace
between us, his two women, and forced us to become
friends. Neither of us was to feel jealous of the other and
the three of us were to travel together from then on.

"When I managed to escape from that situation, I
went back to Stefan. To boredom and to peace. I stayed
away from discos that played tropical music and restau-
rants that served native dishes. I didn't want to meet
anybody, hid behind my foreign husband. Until we
went on vacation.

"And one day during that vacation, just as I was
about to fall from a camel, the camel driver and I
blurted out the same word. And there was no doubt

about it, what I most feared I found there. He'd bounced around from one country to another, worked at every kind of job before ending up as a camel driver. Soon after, he said to me all the words he'd gone so long without sharing. It couldn't be chance that we'd both sung out the same exclamation, it was our destiny. We were destined to meet this way, he told me. And from that one word we'd uttered, he was going to give me everything I wanted, everything I needed.

"I began to time my husband's naps, to long to spend the night away from the hotel. The camel driver gave me the address of an herbalist from whom I could buy certain powders. A bit in Stefan's drink and we'd have the whole night for whatever we wanted to do.

"He was waiting for me outside. My husband was sleeping peacefully in our room. The night was hardly long enough for us. But when I lay down beside Stefan, an hour before dawn, I found his body cold.

"My camel driver listened to the news as if it didn't concern him. He said either the herbalist or I had made a mistake. But that he wouldn't leave me alone now, at the mercy of the police, and that a truck carrying camels was about to leave and would take me away from there. As soon as nobody suspected anything, we'd be together again, far away.

"I gave him all the money I had with me, and never saw him again. At our first stop one of the men grabbed me and the other did what he pleased with me. From then on I traveled bound hands and feet. In a pond they washed my face, oiled my eyebrows and lashes. And when we reached the market where they were going to sell me, I could understand them praising my eyes of a she-camel.

"A small man approached me, pointed to my nose with his whip; he must have given the truckers less money than what I'd paid for my passage. And then I knew that the first one to sell me had been the camel driver.

"My new owner, two bodyguards, and I arrived at a café where they put me out in the patio like the animals, and gave me a viscous liquid to drink with a spicy flavor. All the fatigue of the trek disappeared and I entertained myself watching the play of grapevine shadows on the floor. When I woke up it was night and an old woman standing next to a lamp was shouting insults at me. Camel shit, I understood her to say. The only son of my owner was about to arrive, a university student coming home for vacation. He was very young and I was destined for him on orders of his father.

"The first night we slept together he hardly touched me. I woke at dawn and he was no longer there. On the second night the same thing happened. Ayán would leave me to go to the bodyguards' quarters. But you learn something from so much suffering. The next night I treated him exactly the way all those characters had treated me and he stopped visiting the bodyguards so often.

"I had to get away from there. I begged Ayán to find a way we could make love beside the sea, but instead he brought me an orchestra of blind musicians. I told him I missed the smell of the sea that did not reach our house, and finally succeeded. He let me out. We went to the nearest port where he chose the tallest tower for us and left me shut in there alone.

"I waited for him a whole day and the next day he was dragged back by a sailor, drunk. As a present he brought a bird that began to curse in German the minute it saw me. Ayán handed me the cage and fell in a heap onto our bed.

"Stefan was not waiting for me anywhere. I couldn't go back to our house. But I had to get out of that port, even if I didn't know where to go. So I asked the sailor how much he would pay me for the boy, bird included. When he stopped laughing, I found that Ayán had already sold me. Now I belonged to the sailor, and that very night we set sail for his home.

"Iceland is at the end of the world, but even at the end of the world I found people from here. I became friends with a woman who was married to a professor at the University. We went to bars, talked about men, and we managed to make it happen. We ourselves, with our desires, summoned a basketball coach. Now there were three of us from here at that end of the world, and the third to arrive was a man.

"He had asked for asylum during a plane stopover,

left his team never to return. If such things happened to me even in Iceland, it meant I was condemned to endure them. I've suspected it ever since I was a child, knew it long before I left here. My mother had passed it on to me as a legacy when she set herself on fire because of a man.

"During the season when the birds return after crossing the sea, one exactly like the one Ayán had given me appeared at a window of the house where I was living with the sailor. I heard it swear in German. It looked at me a moment and I felt sure it was Stefan flying inside that bird, sure that he would follow me forever no matter where I went.

"And in Iceland, at the end of the world, I learned that in a certain way men also flee. And you can't flee from someone who's also fleeing without running into them."

That's why she was here in this restroom telling me her story. She was coming back to surrender. She wished me a future meeting with my son, and left, dragging her suitcases.

"A woman is kneeling at the exit, blocking everybody," I heard someone say a bit later.

It was the same woman. She's still there, on her knees, on the floor, not daring to cross the threshold, as motionless as a statue.

A KNACK FOR MAKING RUINS

For Reina María Rodríguez

"When you need to add to the size of your house and there's no courtyard in which to build anything more, no garden, not even a balcony; when you need more room and you live with your family in an interior apartment, the only thing left to do is to lift your eyes and discover that the ceiling is high enough so another level could be fitted in, a loft. In short, you discover the vertical generosity of your space, which allows the raising of another house inside.

"When you've erected the loft and you live, if you can call it that, with a certain amount of comfort with the family, then if your mother-in-law and your wife's niece come from the provinces, ready to stay in your house for a stretch as long as life itself, the only thing you can do is pay a visit to the psychiatrist. Because you dislike your wife's mother so much by now, you can no longer sit at the same table with her, and the same goes for that pest of a niece. And also because, crammed together the way you all are, you're unable to sleep with your wife and that will drive you to divorce, which would be the least of it, to say nothing of madness and suicide.

"The psychiatrist is then going to ask you if you're willing to follow whatever measures he may suggest to you, no matter how weird they may seem. And you say yes, because you want to be cured, because you now consider yourself sick. Can you acquire a young goat, a kid? he asks you. A live one, he adds. Yes, you respond. Buy it and take it to your house, that's what he orders you to do. And come back for another consultation in two weeks.

"To raise a goat in a loft may not be as weird as living with a mother-in-law. You go back to your place with the animal (your neighbors in the apartment house raise pigs and ducks and chickens) and you turn it loose to live with the family. Although living with it becomes impossible right away. For starters it snacks on all the upholstery, your mother-in-law's suitcase, and a housecoat. It shits everywhere, smells like a goat, doesn't let anyone sleep at night. You hold out for one day, on the second day you give the animal some hefty whacks, and on the third you go back to the psychiatrist much earlier than agreed upon.

" 'You have to be nuttier than the nuts who come to consult you. What sort of treatment is this?' you scream at him. And the fact is the treatment begins now, as he explains. 'Now what are you going to order me to do?' you ask him through tears. Get that sacrificial goat out of your house, he says.

"Again you obey, you re-sell the blessed animal (such a quick transaction means you gain nothing) and the next day you're again in the psychiatrist's office. Because you slept well, your wife woke you up at dawn, the sex was as good as ever, and at breakfast, the entire family around the table, you noticed the affection with which your mother-in-law put more coffee into your café con leche. You suddenly understood that life without a goat can be marvelous."

That's how I wanted to begin my thesis about lofts. I hadn't invented the story or read it; it was a real case. The psychiatrist himself had told me the story.

"Do you know what your surname means?" asked the man who was not yet my thesis adviser, as the two of us sat on a bench in the train station.

"Builder," I answered.

"I always envied your grandfather his name."

He was wearing dark glasses to shield his eyes from the light.

"You're going to be a city planner in a family of city planners."

The voice over the loudspeaker announced that the train he was waiting for would arrive in a few minutes.

"And your father cannot help you?"

Until the end of the year my father would be working at a university abroad.

"I imagine you thought of me as you might have thought of your grandfather if he were alive."

I agreed.

"But since I've been retired from the faculty for such a long time, you should look for another adviser.

"And why a thesis about lofts?" he asked.

The train made a clamorous entrance.

"In which direction is this city growing?" I asked him over the din. "Inward, into lofts."

He stood up to scan the people passing by.

"It's growing inward."

Among the crowd of people he picked out a man and hurried to help him with his baggage. He must have introduced me as a student or as the grandson of his best friend, but said not a word to me about the man.

"My car is nearby," he said.

We left the station and I saw the two of them get into the professor's old Soviet auto.

"Let's try it," he said before the sound of the motor could drown out all conversation. "Come by the house."

For years his colleagues at the university had given him up for dead and now seemed pleased that he'd returned to his department.

"Tell me what it's about," he began, ready to get down to details.

The shutters of his apartment were always tightly closed. In broad daylight the leather and gilt of the spines of some books gleamed in the artifical light and the temperature was what you'd find in a cave. As a child I used to visit my adviser in what seemed like another apartment—this same one, but with the shutters open.

"A worthwhile idea," he said.

He was obviously enjoying that moment when we were still free.

"The work will come later," he warned me. "It won't be fun, the editing, polishing, the methodical part."

In that meeting the current could still carry us in any direction; we were swimming like two drunks. My adviser recalled all the cities this city was to be. There was a moment when I thought that if I were to open the shutters, we wouldn't find a city out there.

Alone in the study, I went to examine an ancient street map displayed among the books. It showed the oldest part of the city and carried a date: 1832. As I read that date, I sensed a shadow moving toward the back of the house, and remembered the man who'd arrived on the train.

"There was cholera that year," my adviser explained as he came back from the kitchen, "and they were selling these maps in a shop on the corner of Cuba and Lamparilla."

The map traced the route of the cholera, the advance of death through the city.

The milk formed a cloud in the cup of tea. I wanted to ask whether we were alone in the apartment but didn't dare. As I was saying good-bye I noticed the bowl of coins next to the door. I used to take one every time I came with my grandfather. The coins were from all parts of the world and the one I chose might point toward my destiny.

My adviser also smiled at the memories.

"One more time," he agreed.

I reached into the bowl and took out a metallic button with an anchor in relief.

"From a Navy uniform. It doesn't count, take a coin."

I stirred the contents of the bowl and chose a rough one.

"Let's see where it takes you."

To the touch it seemed to be unfinished.

"For me it rankles above," I managed to read before it was snatched away from me.

In one of the rooms at the end of the hall, an enormous light flashed. My adviser hid the coin.

"It's only a plaything," he tried to convince me. "It's worth nothing."

He opened the door of the apartment and hurried me out.

The shadow in the apartment, the coin, and the flare from behind one of the doors: everything was very mysterious. I raced through the first books, took notes, and a week later rang his doorbell at the hour agreed upon.

In the middle of the door a magic eye opened; someone responded but chose not to open. I pushed the bell again but whoever had been there was gone. I was about to go when my adviser arrived carrying a bag with a bunch of wilted vegetables sticking out. He apologized for being late; his old servant was no longer with him.

The shutters were closed as tightly as during my first visit; behind the door at the end of the hall no light was shining. And I was surprised to find the bowl with the coins in its usual place.

"Rincón," he said handing me a glass of water.

I didn't understand.

"Where they were selling the maps of the cholera route—Rincón's Shop, at the intersection of Cuba and Lamparilla."

We went out to find his car and as we got in I asked about the coin.

"You never noticed that the coins were from different eras," he began. "For a child geography is much more interesting than history. Other countries mean more than other eras . . . Perhaps we still do not need to begin our journeys in time."

"Of course," I said without understanding what connection there could be between this conversation and the coin.

"The bowl at my house is full of money from many places and many eras."

"Yes."

"You don't know where it will end. You go out some morning to buy vegetables . . ."

He stopped before a sign saying Street Closed for Repairs.

"One moment," he said as he got out of the car.

He spoke with one of the workmen, glanced at an open underground hatchway and returned to the car.

"You go out one morning to buy vegetables and discover that cholera is going through the city. In 1832 you went out with no time to be afraid. You need a coin right away, because you know that at Rincón's Shop at Cuba and Lamparilla they'll exchange it for a map that will guide you through that labyrinth."

"What is the date of the coin I picked?" I asked interrupting his digressions.

"It was a plaything, just as I told you. For one of those games where you buy and sell properties."

He had to make another detour because of road work.

"You're no longer the child your grandfather brought to the house. Time, as they should have taught you, is another space. Now it's your turn to explore it."

I felt I'd been cheated out of what was most important. My adviser stopped the car. The silence was incredible.

"I want you to meet someone," he said.

The building we entered had been condemned and no one seemed to be living in it, a most unlikely place to pay a visit. We saw two men removing wooden supports from downstairs and carrying them toward the upper floors. My adviser called at a door with a padlock. A smaller door in the larger one opened and a hand came out and opened the padlock.

We went through the door into a space that could have been the back room of some antique dealer. A sofa bed was the only concession made to a home. There were park benches instead of furniture, the space was subdivided by sections of railing. The lamps were enormous lights for entryways or gates, and street signs hung on the walls. We came upon a man whom my adviser asked about his health.

"Professor D," he introduced me.

"Ex-professor."

He was unrecognizable, although I'd seen him during my first years at the university. Now a chain smoker, he paced back and forth among his belongings and called our attention to a tumbler filled to the brim.

"See that?"

It was the least strange thing there until the water started to move as if stirred by an invisible hand.

"Underground explosions," he explained.

The work crew we'd run across was laying coaxial cable for telephone lines; construction of the subway had been abandoned.

"Air raid shelters," I supposed.

The liquid stopped shaking and my adviser pulled out a package.

"Green," he said. "There was no black."

"Green is good for the enamel."

His teeth were stained from smoking; holding a cig-arette, he rested his hand on my shoulder.

"You see all this stuff?" he asked. "No longer space for it in this city. I took it from a place where nothing will ever be built, but not even I knew what my house would turn into when I brought the first things."

He didn't explain what it had turned into, a flea market or a trash heap. I had to keep the ashes from falling on me.

"In my building a woman began with one aban-doned dog and now there are about fifteen."

He looked at me as if he didn't understand. On the floor above they started hammering.

"I can't make tea because there's no gas," he explained.

The nailing stopped.

"Lofts above and explosions below."

"A miracle to stay alive," my adviser murmured.

"A scandal for all the urban planning conferences," said D.

"A city with so few foundations and one that carries more weight than it can support can only be explained by flotation."

He fell back on the sofa.

"Miraculous statics."

The hammering started again on the floor above and my adviser lifted the tumbler in his experiment to look at it more closely.

"I thought it was water," he said.

"A little more dense, Professor. March rum."

The surface of the rum was covered with dust from the ceiling. My adviser looked up.

"I'd like you to lend your book to this young fellow," he requested at last.

Seated in the middle of his archeological finds, D looked at the burning end of his cigarette.

"But he hasn't told me what he's looking for."

That's how I began with the business of the goat in the apartment.

"He stole a lot of those things before they reached the point of collapsing," my adviser said as we left.

"Don't let any faculty members know," he warned, referring to the book.

It was a typewritten volume of some three hundred pages. The author, the then-professor D, had titled it *Brief Treatise Concerning Miraculous Statics*.

I took special pains to arrive an hour early for the next appointment. Without being seen, I spied on what my adviser was doing in the train station. He was with the guy I'd seen him meet a few weeks earlier. I saw the man hand him something that I supposed to be money. My adviser took it, said good-bye and went to his car. There, he searched for a notebook and wrote in it for a while. After the train pulled out of the station, he went to sit on a bench to wait for me.

However, all my precautions to arrive early and spy on him came to nothing because he told me that he was renting a room in his house to the man. They were involved in some business together; there was no mystery. He stretched his legs as if he felt happy all of a sudden and asked how my reading of the treatise was going.

I'd found a term in the book that might be useful to me.

"If you write *tugurization* in your thesis," my adviser began, "then . . ."

People can overwhelm a building to such an extent they make it fall. Create space where there didn't seem to be any more, push until they have a place to live. And such attempts to live nearly always end up being just the opposite.

People around us were embracing and saying good-bye, helping each other with their bundles.

And on the other hand, there was the determination

of those buildings not to fall, not to turn into ruins. To such a degree that the persistence of an entire city could be understood as a struggle between *tugurization* and *miraculous statics*.

Another train arrived, packed with people.

But if what I wanted was to get my degree in urban studies, city planning, I'd have to forget about such topics because faculty committees would not wish to hear about buildings collapsing. The city still had the same fixed borders; it showed no signs of spreading. When a building fell, they didn't replace it. We took the cheapest way out of a collapse by making a park, or leaving the space empty. Couples found what corners they could, women got pregnant from those trysts, the maternity wards were full, the dead put off dying . . .

My adviser and I watched the train station empty out once more, and saw how waves of *tugurs* kept arriving in the city.

A week later I had a visit from Professor D. They were going to publish his book and he'd come to get it. This hope led him to talk at length about his projects; he lit one cigarette from the end of another and spoke of the volumes to come. He promised to wait until I graduated, then he wanted me to help him with his research; he also wanted my adviser to join him. He talked of forming a research group such as he'd once had. Then, without any apparent cause, he became disheartened, stopped making plans, and even doubted the book would be published as promised.

That's when I heard him mention the *tugurs*. Keeping a cigarette in his mouth and in his somber mood, it was sometimes hard to understand his words, but here is what I managed to catch:

"The oldest buildings in the city attracted the attention of the tugurs. Soon a first tugur moved into a building he'd discovered in his meanders. That first tugur brought others and slowly the building was filled with his people. Once inside a building (the higher the better and the grander better still) they made four rooms out of one small one, and two floors out of one. They drilled into the walls to place crossbeams for their lofts. And the tugur women bred like mad and kept summoning their most distant relations.

"As they went to bed each night, they laid their heads on the pillow, hoping to give the place its final blow. They sought to collapse it by any means. But not to die, because a true tugur causes a building to fall without letting a speck of brickdust fall on him. His victories consist in returning to the house and not finding it standing. You should see them then among people who are really suffering. With the most hypocritical expressions on their faces, they make the victims recount every detail of the disaster."

"Why?"

D didn't seem to understand me.

"Why do they knock the buildings down?" I asked more explicitly.

"They're footloose, rolling stones, they have nomadic blood," he told me. "And it's hard to be like that on a small island.

"Think that the horizon can be reached immediately. Take two steps and you're on the coast, and all the promises made to you as a nomad come to nothing. What your blood tells you every night is a mere mirage of the open road if the land comes to an end.

"So if you can't get out, you go in," he continued. "You're not going to stay put."

Now he was again full of enthusiasm.

"When you find no new land, when you're hemmed in, you still have one recourse: to unearth what's underneath the construction. Excavate, walk on the vertical. Search for the connection of the island with the continent, the key of the horizon."

He lit his last remaining cigarette. We were silent for several minutes.

"Nothing can compare to having the building where you live collapse," he said.

"If your house falls down, you still own the land. You have your corner and can start over."

He looked at the condition of my apartment and seemed to find it too solid.

"But when the apartment building where you've lived all your life falls," he added, "you discover that until then you've had nothing more than air, nothing more than the ability to float unconsciously at a certain height from the ground. And once that privilege is lost, you no longer have anything left."

He smoked his cigarette down until lips and lungs could extract no more smoke.

"Then circumstances turn you into a tugur," were the last words he said, and a couple of hours before dawn he left.

"Do you have the treatise with you?" my adviser had to ask me again on the telephone that same afternoon.

I looked at the clock without seeing the time, cleared my throat to tell him the book had already been returned.

"D came last night and we talked until dawn . . . I just woke up this minute."

"I'm sorry, but D died in a building collapse this morning."

It was almost five in the afternoon.

"The ceiling of his house fell in on him."

I said I'd be at my adviser's apartment as soon as possible. Still not recovered from the news, I remembered the men who'd been removing the wooden supports and hammering over D's ceiling.

He'd been the only one to die.

"They built a loft above him."

"It looks more like suicide," my adviser said very calmly.

The building had been condemned and he chose to run the risk of staying in it.

"I talked with his ex-wife at the identification of his body. It will be best to leave things as they are."

Ex-wife, ex-professor. Now he was entirely settled in the time that seemed allotted to him.

"I'll make some coffee," my adviser said.

I went to the bathroom. Something I couldn't explain, a suspicion, made me push open another door, and going into the room at the end of the hall was like going into another house.

The flooring had been taken up and was now bare unfinished cement. In one corner was a furnace that reached up to the ceiling and in another the old drafting table from my adviser's student days. I went forward, careful to make no noise whatsoever, and then a rope touched my neck.

It was strung from wall to wall with damp pieces of paper hanging from it. Even in the darkness I could see they were bills, paper money. Next to the furnace I found a valise filled with coins like the one I'd picked from the bowl. They were as rough as the floor of the room and must have come from that furnace. My adviser had rented the room to the man from the train station, but not exactly as a place to sleep.

I heard noises outside and barely had time to take a few coins. The damp bills, certainly rare also, remained hanging on the line.

"It was a trick, the business of the book," said my adviser as he handed me a cup.

If they had promised him to publish it, whoever it was that made him such a promise wanted the book to be sunk in the collapse, buried beneath the rubble. He was reasoning now with the reasons of his dead friend.

"I want to show you something," he said in a low voice.

I put my hand in my pocket and felt the stolen coins. In a bookcase, next to the strange map of the cholera, he kept a clothbound notebook. He touched it with a finger and I was about to believe the bookcase would open onto a secret passage.

"If anything should happen," he confided to me, "here are my lecture notes, the only thing left of that book."

"What can happen?" I asked with a not very convincing smile.

The old professor sighed deeply.

"Some sort of accident."

He poured himself a second cup of coffee, something he never did.

"I didn't know," he said, "when I took you there, I mean. When I put it in your hands." I asked what it was he didn't know then.

"All those who've been near that book have come to bad ends," he said.

He counted up people and accidents. Professor D's entire research group had met unfortunate fates. But up until a few hours ago the author of the book was living and what happened could be taken as a chain of coincidences.

"Now you and I are left."

The perfect murder. A collapse that killed the man and also buried the scene of the crime.

"Forgive me."

I asked what I should do with those notes in case something happened.

"Save yourself," my adviser ordered.

In the street, in the afternoon light, I looked at the coins. "For me it rankles above" was written on one side. "For me it rankles below," it said on the other.

After dark when all curious onlookers had left the collapsed area, I was there. A dog was circling about among the rubble looking for something. Someone whistled, a few pieces of the wall were removed, and the dog came out of the tunnel it had dug. In the back, like one of those doll houses with open facades prized by little girls, the one wall that still stood had Professor D's street signs. Then I remembered the title of a book he was planning to write: *A Knack for Making Ruins*. Between becoming a tugur or being dead he'd chosen the latter.

After D's death, the first thing I did every morning was to make sure my adviser was safe and sound. My thesis advanced slowly and the door of the room in the back was never open again. One afternoon I was alone in the study paging through the clothbound notebook when I saw the guest from the back room reflected in a mirror, but when I turned around he was no longer there.

The next morning nobody answered the telephone at my adviser's house. They found him seated in one of the easy chairs in his study, dead. The light came through the windows as it had a long time ago. The notebook was missing from the shelf and the back room held only a drafting table. No trace of the furnace or the false bills.

"Heart attack," was the coroner's finding.

Death seemed to have surprised him in his easy chair while he was resting. The ceiling had not fallen on top of him nor did his body show any signs of violence. He was wearing his reading glasses but had no book in his hands; he'd been paging through the stolen notebook for sure.

"Save yourself," he'd told me.

In a pocket I had the only proof of the strange clandestine work in the back room, and no clear idea of how my adviser had been involved in it.

For several weeks I kept watch around the area of the train station, which meant I had to stop working on my thesis. One afternoon I was on the point of giving up my vigil when I saw my adviser's former guest get off the train.

He was carrying the familiar valise and talking to a woman taller than he was. Unlike other recent arrivals, he was in no hurry. We walked back and forth in futile pacing. His activities were so trifling I suspected he was waiting to meet someone.

After night fell I followed him along an unlit avenue, made even darker by the trees. He stopped before the mouth of a tunnel that must have been the entrance to an air raid shelter. He looked all around without seeing me, opened a grating and went inside.

A car illuminated the place for an instant just as I was about to convince myself that none of it was real, neither the unlocked grating at the mouth of the tunnel, nor the stone wall behind the trees. I followed the stranger without really knowing why.

Inside the tunnel, I paused in order to find sufficient light. I opened a knife I had with me and tried in vain to hear footsteps. The roof was so low I had to walk bent over. Soon the floor became cement and I came to an intersection with another tunnel of larger diameter but in complete darkness.

Some wooden boards indicated the continuation of the path; trickles of water ran along the ground.

"A branch of the subway that won't be built," I said to myself.

The slope grew steeper, the rough cement clung to the soles of my shoes. I thought I heard steps, stopped, but nothing interrupted the silence. The illumination became dazzling and I discovered that the path led into blinding light. It must be another intersection, lit up this time. An arm stopped me; I dropped the knife.

Behind the bars of one of the walls, a woman held
out her arm. I looked at the glint of her dyed hair, the
knife on the ground, and the light at the end, beyond
which there seemed to be nothing.

"For me it rankles above," she said holding her hand
out.

She was clinking a heap of coins like those I had in
my pocket and made an impatient gesture. To placate
her, I put one of those strange coins into her hand.

"For me it rankles above," she repeated without letting me enter.

"For me it rankles below," I completed the password.

If, at so many meters below ground a ticket window
were to open, the scene awaiting me would certainly
not be more strange. I took a step backward; the knife
was nowhere in sight. At the end of the tunnel the light
gleamed brighter than on a sunny day. Once within
such clarity, the space was enormous. Reflectors in the
ceiling hid its existence entirely. Rather a sky of beach,
of radiant summer, opened over my head.

There was almost nothing in that space that seemed
to have no limit. Nobody was in sight and the desola-
tion of such a vast place did not invite exploration. It
would be as boring as walking around a sun. Later I
noticed some lines, a city map traced to natural scale.
And soon I began to see some buildings, here and
there, at a distance from one another. An understanding, the same as the power of sight in the midst of so

much light, would gradually reveal certainties I would prefer not to know. So I attempted to go back.

But it was impossible for me to find an exit. I had arrived in a nightmare city and did not know how to wake myself up. I took out the coins expecting something to happen but nothing did, and for no reason I remembered the corner of Cuba and Lamparilla. Or for even less reason thought of being in that very place but below ground.

If I didn't get out immediately, I would have to accept that a city very similar to the one that existed above ground existed below it. So similar that it must have been planned by those who caused the buildings to collapse. In front of a building lacking one of its walls, I understood that the missing wall, still standing in the world above, would not take long to get here.

It was Professor D's building erected once again. I would have to cross the entrance and search for the door that contained the smaller door, assure myself that everything was the same. Only that way, still more entrapped than if I were to pass beyond a ticket window and advance into such enormous light, would I have arrived in Tuguria, the sunken city, where everything is preserved as in memory.

"But my thoughts are far off with Bethmoora in her loneliness, whose gates swing to and fro. To and fro they swing, and creak and creak in the wind, but no one hears them. They are of green copper, very lovely, but no one sees them now. The desert wind pours sand into their hinges, no watchman comes to ease them. No guard goes round Bethmoora's battlements, no enemy assails them. There are no lights in her houses, no footfall in her streets; she stands there dead and lonely beyond the Hills of Hap, and I would see Bethmoora once again, but dare not."

I heard my grandfather repeat this passage many times. I learned his words without understanding completely, without knowing whether he was alluding to a real or an imaginary city. And as happens with so many citations from memory, its definitive moment came to him some time afterwards, without warning.

AT THE REQUEST OF OCHÚN

"What does elephant meat taste like?" my apprentice asks me in sign language.

Forty years in a butcher shop in the Chinese Quarter meant I had cut all kinds of meat. I was just a boy when I came to work with master Chang. I respected the large knives, and was afraid of raw meat and of what appeared when the animals' bellies were opened. The smell of blood collected in basins in the back room made me feel queasy. Everything I know now, everything I'm trying to teach this mute boy they sent me as apprentice, was taught to me by master Chang.

From him I learned the secret of the butcher of the Emperor Wen-hui. Once every twenty years the Emperor's butcher would prepare to sharpen his knife. It wasn't a magic knife by any means. The metal was perhaps no better than the ones we use, but the knife of the Emperor's butcher didn't lose its edge by cutting because his hand guided it through the spaces that already existed in the meat. To know what will occur from one moment to the next, to sense the slash, to move the hand as if what it was doing had already been done and was inevitable: I learned all that from master Chang.

"To cut is criminal," he would assure me just as he was running the metal through the meat. "A crude act, an offense against heaven."

My master's life flowed by in the same way he cut without cutting. He often repeated an aphorism: "No violence, no raising of eyebrows." He had no children and neither had he known a woman. He once told me that a single erection had settled that once and for all. The master butcher Adolfo Chang lived without incident until the night when he came out of the "Golden Eagle" where they were showing the story of the last Empress. At the exit of the movie theater he ran into three teenagers on the lookout for a uniform suitable for a judo academy. They beat him to death for his clothes.

At that particular time I was in jail. Then the elders of the Chinese Quarter, who earlier had not lifted a finger to allievate my situation, joined forces to get me released. They were not willing to be served by a butcher who didn't know the secret of the Emperor's butcher. And I was the disciple of the dead master, a link in the chain of those who possessed the secret.

"No violence, no raising of eyebrows," I had them inscribe on his tomb.

Since he had no family, they'd buried the master in the vault of a social club he'd never entered. He, who couldn't bear the boasting of those who block the game on purpose, lay at rest among old domino players. All the discretion he'd practiced during his lifetime led to the explosion of his death by violence in the street.

When I returned to the butcher shop, the apprentice who'd replaced me during my years in prison was waiting for me. I saw him cut and realized he had not the slightest hint of the secret. I knew right away he wouldn't last long there.

The late master's lesson of remaining imperturbable also had produced no effect whatsoever on the apprentice. An argument between him and a customer over a quarter of a pound made it clear from the first day. I had to leave my own work and put myself between Ignacio and the customer. The battle over, the quarter pound in question remained in our favor. I don't know what the Emperor Wen-hui's butcher would think of such a thing, but that's how it turned out. We were in the Chinese Quarter. Beef appeared very seldom and the chickens coming from Bulgaria were getting more albino all the time. "You stink worse than a bogomil chicken" became an insult among us.

I quickly understood that Ignacio was able to work without conflict until some accident, or some request, prevented him from thinking about his wife. He needed to think about her all the time. He was recently married. He'd married as an adolescent according to Chinese tradition, not so much to conform to the old customs as to sleep with his sweetheart Lumi every night.

Luminaria Wong, unlike Ignacio, was not completely Chinese. To describe such beauty in a nutshell, Lumi was a Chinese mulatto. The color of her skin varied continually and changed as the color of other women's eyes change. That skin was at its best after dark, for sure.

"Pure gold in cave," my master would have said, if he'd been alive and if he'd had a different nature.

And then, there were her eyes. One could explain Lumi's skin by the mingling of families, but as for the origin of her eyes, something animal was woven into the story. Looking into the eyes of Luminaria Wong one could sense a clearing in a grove and some distant ancestor of hers speaking with an animal as beautiful as a vision. Lumi's eyes came from that animal.

After their marriage, Ignacio tried to make sure that no one else looked at those eyes, that no one else thought about that skin. He wanted his wife for himself alone and tried to keep Lumi at home, without much luck. But the secret of his wife's beauty depended on letting it go free, letting it spread like hearty laughter. When she was christened they'd wanted to give her a name that in Chinese means "The Happiness of the World, and There Is No Other."

f the lost daughter-in-law, fanning out over
uarter like the seer's sticks over the green
ria Wong was not to be found anywhere
. The city extended beyond the Chinese
ountry stretched still farther beyond the
m the first moment of losing her, Ignacio
d never love anyone else as much as he
ia Wong. Nobody in the entire world;
that in the dark mirror of a cow's liver.
ave crossed the sea," he mused standing
k where we threw entrails.
t the shop across the street as if it were
orizon and Lumi were about to emerge
a vision as magical as her flight.
e days I introduced him to my wife's
aughter of the first marriage of my third
at he could knock some sense into her so
n. But nothing happened between them.
ork," my assistant confessed to me the

ot to worry about it, that there were
worked and times when it didn't. From
acio all times were times when it did-
here thrusting a knife into the meat in
rs embarrassed him, so he had to do his
k room.
er to decipher than Chinese writing,"
m after taking just one look at him.

My helper in the butcher shop immediately con-
sulted the seer of the club his family belonged to. In a
small cubicle, beyond the sound of the domino tiles or
the clamor of toasts, he asked the seer for knowledge
about his marriage. The seer had got scandalously
drunk at Ignacio and Lumi's wedding, and Ignacio had
trouble believing in him after that.

He saw him unfold a small green piece of badly
frayed carpet with greatest skill. Heard him decide that
this time it would be better to leave the coins in their
rust and to consult the dry sticks of milfoil. Milfoil,
milenrama, or many leaves, was also the name of
Ignacio's family on account of its many relatives. The
allusion caused Ignacio to regard the seer with more
favorable eyes. He grasped the oracle's bunch of sticks
knowing that the minute he relaxed his hand the
inevitable would happen.

"Work on what has been spoiled," the voice in the
cubicle pronounced.

He immediately tried to explain that it was not nec-
essarily a bad omen but Ignacio now didn't hear him.

"She's been spoiled," he thought of his wife, of Lumi.

The doctrine of the Emperor Wen-hui's butcher
rests on guiding the knife through the spaces that
already exist in the meat. Besides that secret, Ignacio
also knew nothing of how to penetrate the gestures and
thoughts of his wife.

"Spoiled!" he insulted her with the first blow.

After her surprise, Lumi tried to hit him back, only to receive even more blows. Ignacio chased his wife through the entire house until she managed to squeeze herself under the sink.

"Come out or it's going to be worse," he warned her.

While she was crouching there, he couldn't hit her. Lumi begged him to leave her in peace.

"What have I done to you?" she wailed from her hiding place.

What had Luminaria Wong done to him? The same as some annoying customers of the butcher shop, she didn't let him think about his wife. Because it wasn't Lumi who lived with him now. It was someone similar to her who, with gestures, words, wanted to erase the real one. For the last time he asked if she wouldn't come out.

"First you get out," Lumi answered him. "This is my house."

He then nailed some bars across the space under the sink, making her refuge into a prison. And then he left, and couldn't hear his wife's shouts asking him to forgive her and not leave her shut up there.

"Pure gold in cave," master Chang would have said seeing her behind the bars.

Ignacio Milenrama went off to work as usual. At quitting time I invited him to come with me to a warehouse on the edge of the Quarter. An acquaintance

who wanted to ㎜
place of piled up
of rice so no one

"We seem lik
who'd also come

"Happy weevi
while popping of

Ignacio drank ㎜
ourselves remind
out on that poor

"Get your assi
warehouse said to

"You spoiled t
"Next time," h

There wouldn'
the secret of the ㎜
to his house with
running he was s
I couldn't undei
wife's name. I be
love, newly wed,

That night, w
Lumi wasn't the
the way he'd left
gone. It seemed

The Wongs sa
police didn't hav
Milenrama family

whereabouts
the Chinese
carpet. Lumi
in the Quart
Quarter, the
city limits. Fr
knew he wo
loved Lumin
he discovere

"She may
next to the t

He looked
the line of th
from the wal

During th
daughter, the
wife, in hope
she'd settle de

"It didn't
next day.

I told him
times when
then on, for
n't. He got to
front of custe
work in the

"You are
a santero tol

Ignacio had dared to lift his hand against a daughter of Ochún, the goddess of love and happiness.

"Lumi, daughter of Ochún," my assistant began to understand. "The reason for her skin and her walk and her hair down her back and her love of bracelets and those eyes . . ."

Lumi's eyes now seemed to him those of a goddess. He looked into the eyes of the santero and saw Lumi's eyes. They came from far away to confront him, then instantly changed back into the tired eyes of the man he was consulting. The santero had seen the hole beneath the sink and the bars with which Ignacio had tried to cage the daughter of Ochún.

"Heart of elephant," he wrote on a piece of paper for Ignacio.

"The only thing that may save you from the wrath of Ochún," he explained, "is to offer her the heart of a male elephant."

Ignacio didn't take time to consider how odd the request was, he only asked where he should carry the offering.

"Get it first."

The santero's look didn't give much credit to that Chinese boy.

"Later Ochún will say."

"Ochún will return Luminaria to me?" asked my assistant as if he were weighing a business deal.

"Ochún doesn't have her. She is Ochún's daughter."

"And then what do I get out of that heart?" asked Ignacio without opening his lips.

"Ochún has you. And you want to get out of all this."

"And after giving her my offering, can you make sure that she comes back to me?"

The santero would have agreed just as if he'd proposed an appointment sometime during the next two centuries.

"This one will never touch an elephant not even in his dreams," he said to himself.

A heart of a male elephant was Ochún's way of saying impossible.

"And what about the elephant in the zoo?" Ignacio asked the next day.

We were alone behind the counter. I folded the newspaper and looked at him hard.

"There's no elephant in the zoo?" he asked again.

"There was."

"It died?"

"She was killed."

Four of us butchers had got together to kill the female elephant of the zoo. Master Chang, who was still living at the time, knew nothing of the enterprise, but I went off with his knives. We took advantage of a stormy night so the single bullet we'd use to kill her wouldn't be heard by the park guards. After the shot, we had one night to cut her up. One night and one bullet.

To kill an elephant you have to trace an imaginary line that runs from ear to ear. You aim at that line, preferably as near the center as possible. In all our visits to the zoo we took mental aim at the elephant.

The night we chose to kill her was dark with a lot of lightning. None of us felt pity for what was going to happen. More than anything, we were afraid. To kill her without anybody knowing was no minor matter, and on top of that we'd get tired slicing up such a mass. And then we'd have to carry her out. But we were four quick butchers, and the guy with the truck carried the gun.

"With only one package we fill the market," we never tired of repeating.

We'd become rich.

The truck brought us to the street closest to the elephants' pit and we jumped the fence. Beneath the sound of the rain we could hear the animals moving restlessly in their cages. The stormy night was keeping them from sleeping. The elephant was huge, she seemed to be sleeping and was in profile, a bad position for the shot.

A flash of lightning showed us a way down. The ground was softened by the rain. The truck driver would have to go down to the bottom. He looked at us one by one and knew at once that not one of us would go down with him.

"You don't have to take a risk," he muttered.

He was going down the slope and would soon be

ready for the shot, but the rain made him slip. He landed all the way at the bottom, with the rifle a couple of meters away from him. The blow of his fall awakened the elephant and we gave him up for lost. The elephant, however, was old and lazy and wasted too much time taking in what was happening in front of it. Our guy managed to recover the rifle, sense the coming of a thunderbolt, take aim, and bring her down. The animal spent her last moments gazing at the hunter, made a last shortsighted gesture, and fell over dead.

We immediately fell upon her; she was a vast mountain of money. We took two or three turns around her before deciding how to proceed and then one guy had the idea of screwing her.

"Wait a moment. Don't cut her," he asked us.

We had no time to lose.

"It'll be very quick," he assured us. "It's that the females I like best are the fat ones."

He had his pants open and was getting ready.

"While he's doing his business, we'll get started," we agreed.

But the lover of fat females heard us.

"Just a minute," he was already having his way with the animal. "It's bad enough she's dead, you're not going to cut her up on me."

We wasted no time in attacking her flesh. The truck driver, cold-blooded enough for the chase, got nauseated seeing us quarter the elephant with four machetes.

The earth of the pit filled with blood, and as rain fell upon it, fumes of blood rose. An animal meant to destroy jungle is as difficult to cut through as the jungle is to cut down. Aided by lightning we managed to locate the bones and were skinning the giantess when we heard the noise of a motor.

"The truck!" we four butchers yelled in chorus.

In front of me was the reddish throat and I removed the tongue. We raced up the slope slipping at every attempt. Outside the zoo, in the street, no truck was waiting for us now.

Dawn would come as punctually as ever, and there we were with the greatest cargo of meat one could dream of, with no means of escaping with it. We were stuck in a hole, like the defunct elephant in her pit.

"Each one take whatever he can," we agreed.

And we carried out four heavy sacks from the pit. The rain had stopped; it would be light in a couple of hours. What we hadn't counted on, besides the truck leaving us, was the hunger of the other animals. The air cleansed by the rain wafted the sharp smell of the elephant's blood to them in their cages. And they began to roar. All the carnivores in the area were begging us for their share. The animals' hunger gave us away. In prison we also thought the man with the rifle might have betrayed us.

"It wouldn't have worked," Ignacio stated. "It has to be the heart of a male."

I agreed.

"Meat of a male for Ochún."

For a long time after our night of hunting in the zoo, the elephants' pit stayed empty. Not even on the sly could Ignacio get his heart.

One afternoon, he paused in his work with the knife and looked at the shop across the street, his private horizon.

"Africa!" he suddenly shouted.

The two or three customers who were waiting looked at me for an explanation. "I'm going to the war."

For those who might wish to see elephants in the wild, we had our wars in Africa. And Ignacio Milenrama enlisted. War would suit his nature. A good scare, to be near death, a few dangerous memories with which to enliven his later days. The desire for a woman, with no outlet there, would make him desire anyone in place of Luminaria. It may be that Ochún's saying to him "Heart of male elephant" meant to Ignacio: "Go to Africa, put yourself in danger and I'll pardon you." Maybe he wouldn't have to take back the heavy hunk of meat in his army pack.

The elders of the Chinese Quarter promptly sent me another apprentice. He was mute and younger than Ignacio, and perhaps would learn better. For months I heard nothing of my previous assistant. One morning the mute boy brought me a postcard sent by the

Milenramas. Ignacio had scrawled some greetings on it and on the other side was an image of the African desert.

It seemed stupid to me to enlist in a war that condemned him to the desert; that would be useless for Ignacio. A few weeks after the postcard, and a long time since she'd been seen, I saw Luminaria Wong walking along the street. A younger sister was with her. Luminaria glanced briefly at the interior of the butcher shop, looked at the mute boy who was taking her husband's place, and continued on her way. I called to her, but couldn't even get her to turn around. She went so far as to give her younger sister a shove to make her hurry along.

I would have liked to tell her how her husband had felt about her disappearance, show her the wall across the street where he searched for her. They were still a couple of kids, they could forgive one another. For a year I had no more news of my one acquaintance in Africa. Until the day when Luminaria Wong came to the butcher shop with two of her brothers and a package.

The boys put the package on the counter. I noticed that the wrapping carried military seals. Unwrapped by my assistant, an enormous mass of meat lay on the counter. Lumi didn't take her eyes off it, raised them toward me for an instant.

"You know what it means, right?"

I said I did.

"I'd like you to be the one to cut the meat," she requested.

At first the path of the spaces wasn't yet clear for the knife. We had to wait. While the meat thawed, she could tell me what she knew of Ignacio.

At first he'd had some hard months in the desert, she'd heard. Then the war moved closer to the jungle, toward the areas of heavy rains. Ignacio went to bed every night happy to have lived through one more day, and every morning he awoke hopeful that perhaps the new day would bring him his encounter with elephants.

The war, however, caused the elephants to flee. The animals were leaving the jungle to the men. He'd have to get away from the troops to find the trace of a herd.

"Farther on, farther on," the natives said, pointing to the horizon.

In a market among shacks he bought an ivory amulet, a rattle against evil spirits. For two cans of stewed meat he got himself a wide band made of elephant hide.

"When I get the heart, what will I do with it so far from the Chinese Quarter?" he must have asked himself nights when he was on guard duty, more alone with the night surrounding him on all sides.

He found himself in the pit of the war, but he was hearing the voice of the black santero who assured him:

"Get it, then Ochún will say."

One night when it was raining he quit his tour of guard duty early, left the camp and took his weapon with him. Beneath his jacket he had wrapped his torso in the elephant skin and hung the amulet around his neck. He left the war behind to embark upon his true mission, the one that would take him to the big animals.

On his trek Ignacio almost fell into the hands of the enemy and escaped by a miracle.

"Ochún wishes it so," he said to himself.

He traveled long days going ever deeper into the jungle. Wrapped in the skin and protected by the amulet, he penetrated deeper and deeper into the heart of the continent. He kept going until he ran across the trail of an elephant herd and followed it for two days. Then he made a long detour to get ahead of the animals, and waited for them at a place where they would surely stop to drink.

He didn't have to trace the imaginary line of death that in elephants goes from one ear to the other. His first salvo knocked the leader of the herd down onto its knees. All around the earth trembled and the air filled with bellowing. Blood as thick as heavy fabric flowed from the elephant. Ignacio killed the animal with another salvo.

With his knife he searched for the entry to the heart. He could handle the blade with some skill, learned in the butcher shop of the Chinese Quarter. He cut the ligaments and the heart fell onto the blood-soaked grass. Ignacio stepped back a few paces and raised the offering of the heart to the sky over the clearing.

He dedicated it to the goddess with Lumi's eyes.

Now he was at peace with her, and had atoned for his guilt sufficiently. While lifting the heart to the cloudless sky, he saw a helicopter appear. It hovered overhead and over a loudspeaker Ignacio heard his army name.

"Ochún wishes it so." He lowered his offering.

They ordered him to drop his weapon and to give himself up. He left the heart on the grass where there was no blood, looked for a second at the path burnt by the passage of the elephants, discarded any notion of escaping—if he'd had one—and surrendered without protest to the military court that sentenced him to die. He went to his death without amulet and without the elephant skin that had wrapped his torso. He requested only that they grant one wish, his last wish: that they deliver the heart of the dead elephant to his wife in the Chinese Quarter, Luminaria Wong.

"So he died then," I said to the girl.

"Yes."

A puddle had formed around the great ball of meat.

"Dishonorably," Luminaria added.

"He didn't go for the honors," I said to her. "He went to the war because he loved you."

"Yes."

She touched the mountain of meat with a finger.

"Can you cut it now?"

Certainly I could. My assistant understood that he was witnessing an important moment of his apprenticeship.

"Thinner," she asked.

She wanted me to keep a couple of pounds and my assistant was eager to take a bit also. But it seemed to me that the meat belonged entirely to her. That's how it happened that I cut elephant meat for a second time, without ever getting to know its taste. Some days later Luminaria remarked to me that after eating the meat, it had brought her strange dreams.

THE SUMMER IN A BARBERSHOP

I

The facade was still only half painted and in the end would certainly turn out to be gaudy. A wooden board had replaced the pane in the door, since no piece of glass of the same size was available. Like every Friday when I pushed the door open, they changed the topic of conversation. And then after weeks of absence, Ronco was there. He was called Ronco because of his constant hoarseness.

I felt obliged to tell him he was looking better.

"Don't believe it," he answered almost without voice, as he adjusted the handkerchief that covered his throat.

He was going to die soon.

"No coffee," Lilo announced.

A young black man was sitting in the only barber chair in the shop, head tilted forward while Lilo shaped letters into the hair on his neck—three letters: "YGP."

"His initials," Manín explained to me.

The chair whirled around and the black man's eyes stopped in front of me. Too fixed a gaze for him not to have been smoking grass, but not a trace remained in the air of the barbershop.

"They took away the old woman who made it," said Lilo referring to the coffee.

I should have been told about the old woman's arrest, but I didn't know a thing.

The young black man leapt from the chair, the three letters on his neck.

"Less work for Argelio," said Lilo as he closed the door.

Manín and Ronco looked at me as if I were hiding the whereabouts of the old woman who made the coffee.

"Who is Argelio?" I asked Lilo.

"The prison barber."

"And that woman with the coffee, isn't she your wife's aunt?" I asked Manín.

He answered that nobody in his mother-in-law's house knew anything.

"We're screwed then," I concluded.

Ronco began laughing, sounding like a bellows.

"Sit down here, come on."

Lilo led me to the barber chair. The old woman had gone up in the hills to look for coffee. That's all. And anyway it was summer, the first Friday of the summer, and Ronco had come back from one of his hospitals; the air conditioning wasn't cooling the shop much, and a few beers would be better than coffee.

"Where's the beer from?"

Manín was collecting the money. Beer was beer, every single one of the bottles sealed; we'd drink them just as they would arrive from the brewery. I asked to be in on the purchase.

"Don't you dare move from here!" Lilo ordered.

Manín turned left as he went out. Lilo lit a cigarette, and a deep drag drew in the cheeks of his goat face.

"Exactly the way I would have done it," said Ronco's eyes focused on the cigarette.

When a couple of policemen opened the door, Lilo simply threw me a glance.

"I'm busy with this one," he pointed to me. "Come back tomorrow."

The two policemen hesitated a moment, looked my way, and left. Lilo stopped them for a moment to ask if Argelio was still the prison barber. He was.

"It's such a small world," Ronco said, "no bigger than a handkerchief," and again touched the one that covered his throat.

Lilo and Ronco seemed comfortable with me. Any contraband deal—a few beers for example—would be spoiled because the police themselves know and respect me. But with me they felt secure.

When Manín unwrapped the beer bottles, Lilo hid

them in the machine for warming towels and Ronco quickly filled the coffee pot and cups.

"In case of an inspection," he started to warn Lilo, but his throat filled with foam.

"We'll say it's coffee," Manín finished the sentence.

"Vietnamese tea," Lilo answered.

"Call it Vietnamese," said Ronco, "but it is life itself."

Considering that the brewery was six hours away by car and that the warehouses where the trucks made their deliveries were near the port, and that Manín veered to the left when he went out of the barbershop and took no more than ten minutes to bring them, one could figure that those beers . . .

"This one was a santero," Ronco began. "Lilo, you must have known him when he lived in your neighborhood."

Lilo and Ronco immediately placed the guy's identity, like one more bit of contraband, so that I didn't catch his name. Yes, Lilo knew him by sight and now realized how much time had gone by since he'd been seen.

"Because," Ronco explained, "that man is no longer here."

In his mouth the sentence sounded funereal.

"If I tell you where he lives now, you're not going to believe me."

"Where?" Manín asked as he opened the door of the towel warmer.

"I'll have to tell the story from the beginning," Ronco said.

"Manín, careful, don't shake it," Lilo warned him.

"And even when I tell you the whole story, you won't believe it," said the raspy voice.

"Then don't tell it, Ronco," said Manín.

But Ronco was already doing as he pleased.

"This santero had a huge altar in one of the rooms of his house. Without knowing anything about carpentry, he had made the altar with his own hands. And without knowing anything about sewing, he'd made the saint's clothes and his cape. Even when such things couldn't be found anywhere, not even in dreams, he searched for a string of little lights for him. And thanks to a Greek ship, he managed to get an apple. A red apple, real, Greek. And he put the apple as an offering on the altar and when the apple gave the first hint of rot, he covered it with varnish so no bug could get inside it.

"Over time, with each layer of varnish to preserve it, the apple became less red, and little by little took on the color of the wood of the altar. It looked more like a wooden apple than a live fruit, almost nothing remained of the fiery red of the peel."

Ronco looked at me for a second before continuing. I guessed that now would come the tricky part of the story. "The life of the santero was the same as that apple placed as an offering on the altar. The peel of his heart was disappearing, turning into wood, and he had to make up his mind."

"I don't understand," Manín interrupted.

"Well, the guy wanted to leave," Lilo answered immediately.

"He wanted to leave, yes. He had to get out secretly, outwit the vigilance of the coast guard and face the odyssey of the open sea. Without knowing anything about carpentry, he had to invent his own raft. And soon he was sure that he should make it with the very wood of the altar, with those same boards."

"He didn't have any other wood," Manín supposed.

"The saint, on the other hand, didn't want to move from where he was. He preferred the offering of the embalmed apple to all the fresh apples the voyage might bring him. And he announced to the santero that all would go well with his adventure as long as he was left in good hands."

Ronco stopped his story for a moment to drink a cup of beer. A customer came in and Lilo got rid of him with the excuse that he was cutting my hair and then would do the others.

"The day he picked to escape, he went to say farewell to the altar he'd built knowing nothing about carpentry, and to the image he'd clothed knowing nothing about sewing. He'd finally found other wood to reinforce an inflated inner tube, and took off."

At the very moment the santero was leaving the

coast, a woman with bleached blond hair came into the barbershop. Ronco stopped telling the story and Lilo got busy with my hair.

"It'll be free," he whispered into my ear.

And he started really cutting, because time for the inspection had come. I made as if to get up, but he held me with a bony hand on my shoulder and the open scissors in front of my nose.

"Dalia," Lilo said in greeting.

She looked at the one remaining mirror of the three the shop once had.

"Why me?" I muttered to the barber.

Lilo turned the chair around.

"Look at yourself," he seemed to answer me.

And in the mirror covered with damp spots, there we were. Inspector Dalia and me.

"There's a mirror in the office that might be useful to you," she said the moment she saw me. "I'll send it over."

"That would be very good," Lilo replied.

Dalia tried the buttons of the air conditioner.

"And a serviceman for this equipment," she promised in front of me.

"Don't cut it too short," I said to the barber.

Our unanimous prayer for that woman was "May she not try to repair the towel warmer."

"Are they treating you well?" she asked me very respectfully.

Manín in a low voice asked for the continuation of the story.

"Prison," I thought I heard Ronco say.

"Fly droppings," she poked a finger with a red nail into one of the corners. "And what are you drinking here?"

The scissors clacked perilously close to my right ear.

"Vietnamese tea," Ronco said at last.

Dalia looked at the handkerchief that covered Ronco's throat.

"Would you like to join us?" Manín had the nerve to ask.

You could have heard any one of the flies in the barbershop shit. If Manín went this far it was because I was there. Dalia refused her cup of beer, the scissors closed, and my ear was still intact.

"Everything's fine, Lilo," she said as she was leaving.

"The santero left for the north on his raft, with full confidence in his luck, his saint, and in a few hours he was intercepted by a coast guard cutter and ended up in prison."

Prison was not a very unusual place for a story such as this to end, so he had to keep going.

"He spent years in prison. The scarier the nights are in the countryside, the more ghost stories people tell. In prison, when people get together to tell stories, the tales they hear are about people who manage to escape."

From the glance that Manín and Lilo exchanged I could guess what they were thinking: Here, we were always listening to the same stories as the prisoners, just like prisoners too.

"And in prison, the santero listened to stories of those who, unlike him, had managed to escape. The one about the watchmaker who — with the patience watchmakers have — went to the coast every day to fly a kite, calculated the winds, and escaped at last on a raft, flying the huge kite as sail. The one about the man who rented a yacht to celebrate his birthday with his entire family, and to threaten the captain, he carried a pistol inside the cake, and when the captain told him he didn't have enough fuel to get out of territorial waters, he ordered that the bottles be opened because he'd filled them with fuel. . . . And the one about the rider who smeared his horse with tar and bound divers' flippers to his hooves and . . . "

"Ronco," Manín broke in, "you've already told us all those stories."

"Yes, all those stories," there was a tone of farewell in his voice. "And while the santero was listening to all those stories, he said to himself that when he got out of there, he'd try again. Because there was no power in heaven or earth that would prevent him from going wherever he wished to go. And if the kite-flying watchmaker and the man with the birthday cake and the rider . . ."

"All those people," said Manín.

"Fill up my cup and stop being a pest," Ronco answered. "He, too, would succeed. So the day his sentence was up, the first thing he did when he got out of prison was to look for a whip, and with the whip he confronted the altar with its saint. He loosened the very boards he'd once fitted together and, when the boards fell to the floor, he assaulted the image with blows of the whip. No matter how the figure leapt from one of his lashes, he went after it again with the tip of the whip. He demolished the cape and the clothes and stopped only when he saw the severed head. The saint's head, loosed from the body, now seemed as dry as the old apple. And he kept stomping his feet against the floor until both apples, the fruit, and the head let out a dry sound, as dry as the crack of an improvised raft against the coast guard launch."

The silence in the barbershop was like the silence when the inspector was offered the cup of tea.

"Now that he'd carried out his vengeance, he decided to leave. This time he'd go from the south and there wouldn't be any raft. He would battle alone with the sea. He covered his body with tar like the rider had smeared his horse, and plunged in, hoping that in waters distant from the coast, some foreign ship would pick him up.

"It was a beautiful day, the water slid in a marvelous way between his arms, and after several hours of swimming, his arms and legs were part of the water. Whoever might see his head among the waves would take it for a loose buoy drifting away. More hours passed, almost a day, until the swimmer had the luck to meet up with a ship."

"With which flag?" Manín asked out of professional interest, because he worked as a harbor pilot.

"Haven't I told you the story about the three people who thought they'd been saved and the ship with the Swedish flag?"

"Another day, Ronco," Lilo said. "Now finish with the santero."

Manín asked again about the flag.

"The yacht was enormous and carried the English flag, and they brought the santero on board with the same curiosity they'd have had if he'd been a tropical fish. For those on the yacht he was the most curious of fish, and they conversed by means of signs, but he managed to say thanks in English and knelt at the foot of a portrait of the Queen of England hanging in one of the salons of the yacht."

"So the guy ended up in England," exclaimed Manín and Lilo.

"That yacht had crossed the Atlantic. It would go through the Panama Canal and head northward in the Pacific, where it would pick up its owner. They allowed the santero to stay on board but the final decision of what to do with him would be made by the owner."

"And who was the owner?"

"A millionaire. An English millionaire, for sure."

"The Queen of England," Ronco announced.

None of us could believe it.

"The santero couldn't believe it either when he found himself before the Queen he'd seen in the portrait. And couldn't believe his luck when the Queen of England decided that he should stay with them on the yacht."

"Swindled by a saint and saved by a queen," said Lilo.

"What swindle?" exclaimed Manín. "If it hadn't been for the saint he never would have run into the queen. First he sent him bad luck and then good luck."

"The santero thought that his story would now be told in the prisons and no others would turn out to be more incredible," said Ronco breaking into the discussion. "Not the one about the watchmaker with the kites or the one who found a pistol in his birthday cake. . . . All those stories."

"So he lives in England now?" Lilo asked, the only one of us who'd known him.

"He doesn't exactly live there," stated the raspy voice. "It so happens that the guy is the personal santero of the Queen of England."

Then I decided to ask his name.

"His name was changed over there, so now he has an English name."

"He was born again."

"Exactly."

The beer was now gone. None of the arguments Lilo gave me in front of the mirror could convince me that my haircut suited me very well. In the usual Friday report I alerted my superiors to the new contraband.

II

"Listen to me, because this is the last story I'll tell you," Ronco warned us three months later.

It wasn't that he might be dying, but he was called to return to one of his hospitals. The summer was coming to an end. It was raining. It wouldn't be long before the first hurricane of the season would be forming somewhere in the area. The facade had been completely painted in a gaudy color, but neither the promised mirror nor the air conditioning repairman had been there. According to Ronco, on an afternoon like this one it would be good to travel far away, he could feel it in his throat.

"This one was a boy from an African tribe," he began.

"Africa," said Manín as he came in.

Our usual group was there, and one other man, a stranger who'd come running in and was waiting for the rain to stop.

"His father had died in the war, and in obedience to the laws of the tribe, his mother became the twenty-sixth concubine of the king. That is, she ceased to be his mother to become royal property, one of the possessions of the chief. The boy had no luck. His father had died and now his mother was dead as far as he was concerned."

The stranger looked at everybody except me. It suddenly seemed to me that I'd seen him somewhere.

"Coffee?" he asked, surprised when Manín gave him a cup.

"The boy was alone, but we're all alone, right? And it went on like that for several years and the boy, now a young warrior, began to live the life of a man. The exact same way his father had lived before he died. That is, the life of an animal in the jungle: forever wary, always alert."

The door opened, perhaps pushed by someone else who was coming in for shelter. However, the wind that had opened it now closed it again.

"A lion, that's what he tried to be. Campaign after campaign, he sought to gain the power his father had enjoyed, to be a great warrior. And even more power than his father, the power of a king. Because one day it occurred to him that he could become greater than the king of his tribe."

"That was his ambition," the stranger commented.

I think none of us liked the fact that he had taken advantage of Ronco's pause to speak up.

"Hasn't it stopped yet?" I asked.

He was the one closest to the door and he opened it

a crack with the tip of his shoe. He waited a moment, until I could see how wet the street was getting, and let the door close. I then noticed his shoes, like a pair I'd had once.

"What the young warrior wanted was simply to dethrone the king of that tribe. And there was only one way, not a matter of being a better warrior or of conversing face to face with the dead and the souls of things, as the elders of the tribe did. No. To be a greater king than the king he merely had to amass a larger fortune. A fortune in Africa."

"Ivory and gold," said Manín.

"Diamonds," Lilo added.

I said "arms," and the stranger didn't look at me.

"Nothing like that, the fortune of that king consisted of some gadgets, junk, a conglomeration of useless things, the treasure of any poor child in another place."

"Gadgets like what?" Manín wanted to know.

"A portable telephone thrown into the trash, a radio with no batteries, the steering wheel of a car. A pile of crap."

"Crap?"

Manín could make that telephone work, build a car to go with the steering wheel.

"A pile of crap such as could not be found for kilometers around. Not to mention mirrors and umbrellas and lenses that changed the color of the king's favorite concubine's eyes.

"And the young warrior quickly realized that no greater treasure could be found among any of the neighboring tribes, such treasure would never turn up as war booty. And that he could only attain it by getting near the whites. So he left the tribe and began his journey toward the lands of the whites.

"He traveled for weeks and weeks, months. He crossed rivers and stretches devastated by fire. Finally he arrived at the whites' first garbage dump. A single glance would have filled the ambition of anyone else right there. But the young warrior who'd escaped from his tribe said to himself that if such treasures abounded there, thrown beneath the heavens, at the borders of the life led by the whites, they were worth the same as the abundant fruits of the jungle. And he figured that what the tribal king kept was a bonanza for monkeys, neither more nor less. So he determined to find out where the true riches were, and kept going, farther and farther on, until he came upon a diamond mine."

"There!" we all shouted, except for the stranger.

Because we trusted that the young warrior's intelligence would help him succeed.

"The mine had an owner, of course. But finding a diamond mine meant he'd have to work in it until he was exhausted, like a slave. But in the end, he was the happy owner of a certain number of diamonds. A small cargo." Ronco's tongue seemed to caress those stones as if they were food.

"How did he steal them?" asked the stranger.

"Open the door to see if it's still raining," I said to him.

He ignored me. I opened the door myself and the barbershop was filled with cooler air than the old air conditioning unit could have generated.

"It's stopped," I said for his benefit.

"Go find coffee, Manín," Ronco ordered.

"First tell me how the black guy got hold of the diamonds."

"But that's not the story."

If he hadn't been about to go back to the hospital, Ronco would have made a story out of that robbery too. The stranger leaned out into the street pretending to breathe the fresh air and I noticed he was checking out the route Manín took to get the coffee.

"It doesn't matter how he came by those diamonds," Ronco said as he picked up the story. "The biggest thing is that he returned to the tribe where for years he'd been given up for dead and now they found him unharmed, returned from a hunt of which only he knew the details.

"Back in the tribe his mother had died and the king continued to add to the number of concubines without giving a thought to his own death — even more reasons for the young warrior to get rid of him. So he displayed his collection of diamonds before the tribal elders and waited for them to decide who should rule over them.

"The elders were a group of old men that death had forgotten, due to a pact they'd made with her. People both powerful and cowardly, and the political future of the tribe depended on them. They looked at the cargo of diamonds, at the clothes the returning member of the tribe was wearing, and burst into carefree laughter. What kind of treasure was that?"

"The other was better," the stranger said as he finished his cup.

Clearly he was trying to find out if both batches of coffee had come from the same contraband.

"Go on with your story, Ronco," we begged him.

"In the eyes of the elders, the diamonds of the young pretender were worth less than the smallest of the king's mirrors, a mirror from a lady's compact. Not to mention the large one, in which the king and a few elders could fit full length. The disapproval of the council of elders was obvious. The king took one of the diamonds and seemed to appraise it. He looked through it and felt less surprised than he did by the change of color in his favorite concubine's eyes. The diamond was not as valuable as a pair of contact lenses. Finally he threw it onto the ground at the place the tribal authorities had allotted for stones, and soon the head of the young arrival from the land of the whites would also roll.

"But at the very moment when the soldiers of the royal guard were about to lay hands on the youth, he made a clear slash across the image of the king in the largest mirror. The king was split in two and this was taken as a sign of ill omen by the elders. That was his downfall.

"Now the youth was the most powerful chief of all the land up to the boundary of the whites' territory. His treasure was millions of times greater than that of the previous king; the royal concubines were now his. However, ambition would not allow him to rule peacefully. It would now carry him farther away from the jungle, farther than the first garbage dump of the whites, farther than the mines and the barracks where he'd slept so many nights crammed in with other workers, farther than the cottages for the engineers and the quarters for the engineers' wives, beyond the sea . . ."

"But where's he going, the black guy?" Manín asked.

"New York," Ronco answered him. "He could choose no other place."

"Why?" asked the stranger before we could.

"To find out where the true riches were. He was moved by the same impulse that had caused him to leave the tribe, his dissatisfaction with the first trash heap of his journey that kept him going to the heart of the treasures. He went to New York because he considered it to be the great diamond mine of white men.

"But the cause is of little importance, because more peculiar than the reason for that voyage was what the new king did on his first stop."

"Where?" Manín asked.

Ronco touched the handkerchief around his neck as if it were hard for him to speak and slowly lifted the index finger of his left hand toward the ceiling.

"Miami?" Lilo and Manín asked in chorus.

"You've said it," Ronco agreed.

"Lilo," I called.

"Wait, wait with the story," said the barber as he followed me to the back of the room.

"Hey, what's going on?"

"I want you to answer me one thing," I said in a low voice. "Honestly."

"Honestly."

"If you had to send someone to buy beer, would you send that guy?"

The stranger was waiting impatiently for the story to continue.

"Manín would go," Lilo assured me.

"Suppose Manín were not here."

"Ronco then."

"And if Ronco weren't here either?"

Lilo looked at him and then at me.

"I'd better go," he said.

"You wouldn't send that guy, right?"

"Of course not," he said finally.

Now Lilo looked at my head.

"It'll seem odd to you that I can know something like that," he began to confess to me, "but the barber who cuts his hair cuts yours."

We returned to the group, to the story. Just as before, the stranger avoided looking at me.

"Already before leaving for the trip to New York, in the midst of preparations, the young king had asked himself what role a retinue of members of his tribe could play in the far-off land of the whites. Savages who don't even know how to put on clothes, he thought. And he put the power of the tribe into the hands of the elders and left for New York with no retinue or body-guards or warriors. Isn't there any more coffee left?"

"Ronco, you've already had six cups," Lilo scolded. "You're going to be sick."

"I'm already sick. The last, or I won't go on."

They served him what was left in the pot.

"There's nothing more like a dethroned king than a king without a retinue," he began. "He has no majesty, no respect; the young king of the diamonds knew that and as soon as he got to the North . . ."

"To Miami," said that guy, the intruder.

"You've said it. The minute he arrived he understood that he had to have a retinue, people who would represent his dominions, his subjects. So he began to hire people the same way he'd seen hands hired for the mines or as bearers for difficult treks. And the ones he hired— and now comes the good part— were blacks from here."

"Blacks from here who were there," Manín's laughter echoed through the shop.

"Ah," Lilo shouted, "here we come in."

Because like every one of Ronco's stories, this one might begin in an African jungle but sooner or later would involve people from here.

"So as not to tire you," but it was Ronco who seemed more tired, "the king dressed our blacks in the gala clothes of the tribe and took them to New York as part of his people. The people from here surrounded him as happy as in a masquerade ball. They thought they were in a Tarzan movie, they so enjoyed themselves."

Manín pushed the barber chair with his foot and made it whirl.

"And when the time came to return to Africa, one of his hired subjects, one of our people, wanted to accompany the king, to go live in the jungle, and he was named adviser to the tribe."

The intruder asked the whereabouts of the tribe and of the newly named adviser. With his eyes fixed on me, as if this question were only acceptable coming from me, Ronco responded.

"He no longer has the name he once had. He no longer has any name. For the time being they call him by the title of Adviser, but we have to let time run its course. Then they'll call him King."

It was, truly, Ronco's last story. In the summary I wrote for my superiors, I made note of the fact that we could now count on a man soon to be a king in Africa, and another very close to the Queen of England. Both could be of use to us from their respective courts. I also pointed out that it was not necessary for them to send anyone else to the barbershop to do my work.

"The compañero who visited the barbershop," they notified me in response to my report, "was part of an inspection we were carrying out."

Everything turned out positive in that inspection. I had faithfully reported what the people in the barbershop were thinking, what their comments were, and about the contraband. My superiors knew through me what could be expected of them at any given moment. I would soon find out where they sold contraband beer in that neighborhood. What I was never to know (but this did not bother my superiors or any of the inspectors at all) was where Ronco got his stories. Because neither Lilo nor Manín could tell me on all the Fridays we had without him later on.

EPILOGUE

PLEA FOR THE HEAD OF MAZARINO

The *Brief Treatise Concerning Miraculous Statics* was lost in a building collapse; all that remains of that book are the few notes given here. No catalogue of publications by demographers, sociologists, or urban planners makes any mention of the tugurs and their hidden city. And the fate of Professor D continues to be an initial, still unmentioned as a reference.

The case witnessed by the woman in charge of the airport restroom, a syndrome similar to the one in Stockholm and the one that affected Stendhal in the midst of the pictorial riches of Italy, is today a subject of study. Medical and psychological congresses have gone so far as to call it, provisionally, the Boyeros Syndrome, after the name of the region where that airport is located.

The recommendation that an imaginary line should be traced from ear to ear before shooting may be found in an essay by George Orwell, titled "Shooting an Elephant." And the end of a story by Lord Dunsany provides the final words of "A Knack for Making Ruins."

Lastly, this epilogue pleads for the head of Cardinal Mazarino on which the Parliament of Paris put a price during La Fronde.

Separated from the body, just as Scheherazade's came so close to being on many nights, it was worth fifty thousand escudos for the person who handed it over. The Cardinal's library had been given that same value and the money from the sale of his books would serve to pay his executioner.

At the time, according to the historical note given above, a head was worth the same amount as the library it had managed to assemble. Reader, it remains for me to wish that this volume may contribute something should a price ever be put on yours.

Havana, December 1998

CITY LIGHTS PUBLICATIONS